Skeleton Cave

By CORA CHENEY

Illustrated by Paul Galdone

SCHOLASTIC 

BOOK SERVICES

Published by Scholastic Book Services, a division of Scholastic Magazines, Inc., New York, N. Y.

☆ ☆ ☆

7th printing .... February 1967

Printed in the U.S.A.

For

WARING and IRENE PARTRIDGE

CHAPTER 1

IT HAD rained for three days. Davy had waded out to the cow shed to feed and water and milk old Bessie every day. Water stood in the furrows between the rows of vegetables in the garden.

Although it was June, Davy built a fire in the fireplace and pulled Grampy close to it, for the dampness had made the old man's rheumatism worse. Ma wrapped his sore leg in an old quilt and sighed gloomily that the crops would be ruined.

Poor Mrs. Cobb, no wonder she sighed. Her husband, Davy's father, was away in the Veterans' Hospital, having his arm treated for a few months. And poor old Grampy's rheumatism was so bad he couldn't walk, and Davy was just a little boy for all the chores that fell on his ten-year-old shoulders. Mrs. Cobb had to run the farm with only the help of the kind neighbors who did the plowing for her.

Then here came all this rain that made the farmhouse seem damp and cheerless and was probably ruining all the fruit and the garden and the cotton.

But Davy whistled and Grampy smiled. In fact, Davy and Grampy behaved as though they liked the rain. They seemed to share a cheerful secret that almost annoyed Mrs. Cobb. How could anyone be happy over such weather? She sighed again, more deeply.

"Looks like we should have brought in two of everything from the barn and turned our house into an ark, like Noah," chuckled Grampy.

"It's nothing to make jokes about, Papa," replied Mrs. Cobb a little sharply. "It looks like it might be a flood."

"Oh, yes!" cried Davy joyfully as he gazed out the window, "the bottom pasture's flooded now, Grampy."

"I tell you it's nothing to be happy about," scolded Mrs. Cobb.

Davy and Grampy exchanged a secret grin.

The fifth day came in with warm, glowing sun. Davy leaped from his bed and ran to help Grampy to the breakfast table. Ma was cheerful, with the sun beaming in the kitchen door, as she put grits, heavy slabs of bacon, and fat, hot biscuits before the hungry boy.

"I'm going to get Bessie into the pasture this morning, Ma," said Davy, gulping his breakfast.

"Get me a mess of greens from the garden first, son," asked his mother, "and get Grampy to the rocker on the porch."

"Yes'm." Davy jumped up from the table and ran into the garden. He quickly filled a basket with tender turnip greens that Ma would cook with a little meat for dinner.

When he returned to the house, he helped Grampy hobble out to the porch.

"I'll get to the cave soon as I get Bessie settled, Grampy," whispered Davy. "I've got my flashlight." He proudly patted his bulging pocket. His flashlight was his prized possession. Pa had given it to him for Christmas, two years ago.

Grampy nodded and smiled. "Hope a lot of

things have washed up in the cave, sonny. Now you be careful. Can you hand me my Bible?"

Davy handed the old man his heavy Bible and ran toward the barn. As soon as he had Bessie ready

for the day, he hurried down the hill to the bottom pasture. The spring had flooded and filled the lowland with water. The water was receding already, and Davy found his way on solid ground to the spring.

He skipped around the rock-edged pool and between two large boulders that jutted out of the base of the hill from which the spring flowed. He entered the cave.

Davy turned on his light and flashed it into the interior of the cave. The sand floor was sopping wet. He let out a low cry when two bats rose swiftly, frightened by the light. He stood still near the entrance, training his light over the floor to be sure no snakes were coiled there ready to strike.

He moved in cautiously as his eyes grew more accustomed to the darkness. Suddenly he stopped his searching light and moved forward, forgetful of snakes, forgetful of bats. His skin crawled eerily at the sight before him.

There, half visible in the shifted sand, was a human skeleton!

Davy stood for a minute frozen with fear. Then he turned and ran from the cave.

"Grampy! Grampy!" he shouted as he ran up the hill, his breath coming in great pants. "Grampy and

Ma! There's a *skeleton* washed up in the cave! The skeleton's come up from the sand!"

And the shaking Davy dropped in an exhausted heap onto the porch steps.

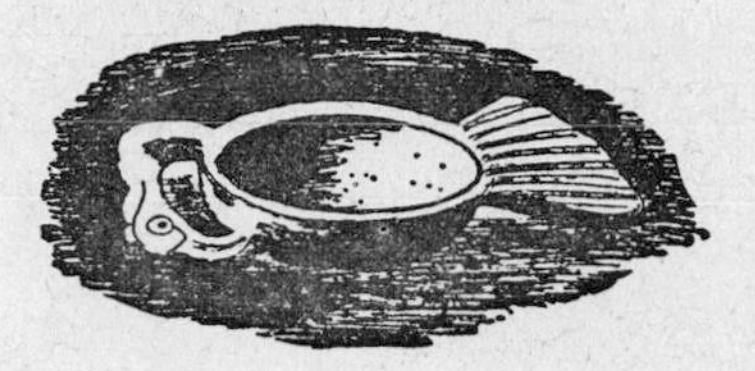

CHAPTER 2

MRS. COBB came running in from the kitchen with her dishtowel in her hand. Grampy tried to rise, and the heavy Bible fell from his lap onto the floor with a thud.

"There," cried Mrs. Cobb, "skeletons in the cave and the Bible falling on the floor! It's bad luck, that's what it is. Get up from there, Davy. What do you mean, you found a *skeleton?*"

"I did, Ma, in the cave. An old skeleton's been

washed up in the flood. He's lying there, Grampy, right in the far corner, with about half of him sticking up through the cave floor." Davy had risen from the steps and was now standing before Grampy, addressing himself to the old man.

Grampy leaned forward with excitement.

"Any dishes wash up, sonny? Any tomahawks or arrowheads? That must be the old Indian skeleton for sure!"

"I didn't stop to see anything else, Grampy. I just flashed my light around to see if there were any snakes, and two old bats flew up to scare me. Then I saw this here skeleton sticking up in the sand, in the far back corner toward the left. I could tell that a lot of sand had washed out of the cave and that the floor was lower."

Mrs. Cobb, with the dishtowel still clutched in her hand, sat down in a straight hickory-bottomed chair that stood against the wall. With her back as straight as the chair, she sharply broke into the excited conversation between her father and her son.

"Davy," she announced with unaccustomed firmness, "you're not to go to that cave again. We have troubles enough with your Pa gone and Grampy sick. No, you got no business in that cave without your Pa or your Grampy."

"Oh, Ma, please," began Davy.

"And you're not to say any more about that skeleton," she continued, "not to anybody. You leave that skeleton where he lies 'til your Pa gets home. Meantime, I don't want folks to get word of it. Promise me, Davy."

"But, Ma," Davy turned an anguished face to his mother, "I *got* to go back and see the skeleton. I *got* to, Ma."

"No you don't *got* to, Davy. You've got to mind me. I never did think much of your going in that cave. There're bats and snakes, and rocks might fall on you. Besides, folks always said it was haunted. Now I know it is," Mrs. Cobb finished with deep conviction.

"Can't I even go with Grampy?" pleaded Davy.

"How could Grampy get there?" demanded his mother. "He can hardly even walk to the kitchen. Yes, you could go with Grampy if his legs would carry him, but I can't and you can't carry him. So you stay out of there until your Pa gets back."

"Now, daughter," Grampy began gently, "don't you think—"

But he stopped at the sight of her face. He seldom opposed his daughter's wishes. She was deeply troubled with the heavy responsibilities of the farm, since her husband was away. Her task was not easy, with himself to care for and only young Davy to help with the work.

"Yes, Davy," the old man turned sadly to the boy, "you must do what your mother says. We won't speak any more about it."

"All right, Ma," he answered heavily, "I promise."

CHAPTER 3

SKELETON CAVE lay in the base of one of the low mountains called the foothills of the Appalachians. Actually the cave was composed of three giant limestone and sandstone boulders. In prehistoric times these had pushed together so that two rocks comprised the sides and a third provided the back and top.

To see it from the outside one would hardly guess there was a cave there, for the narrow entrance between the rocks was not too evident. Dirt had gradually covered the tops, and trees had grown down the mountain sides. So now the rocks seemed merely to poke out of the base of the mountain.

At the very entrance of the cave, the spring bubbled up and formed a little stream that fed into the low-lying pasture beyond. The chamber of the cave was not large, probably not over thirty by sixteen feet. The floor was sandy and damp, and in the springtime when the rains came the little bubbling spring would flood the cave and shift the surface of the sandy floor.

When Grampy was just a little boy, he came with his parents from Tennessee down to the fertile land of North Alabama. They settled on this very farm. It was a good farm because it had the spring and the rich pasture.

But even then the cave had a bad name. Folks said it was haunted, because someone had found a skeleton there once. Of course that was so long ago that nobody really knew, but that was what folks said. However, most people didn't even know about the cave.

When Grampy was a young man, he used to slip into the cave after the springtime flood and find the floor disturbed by the high water. Once he even found an Indian jug, which had been brought to the surface of the shifted sand.

Grampy took a stick and dug about a little more. Gradually he unearthed other Indian relics—a tomahawk, a few odd vessels, some arrowheads. A natural shelf of protruding rock ran across one side of the cave, and on this Grampy placed his treasures. Over the years Grampy added to his store of Indian relics.

Davy remembered the first time Grampy took him into the cave. He had been six years old. And he'd gone to the spring with Grampy and had found the opening in the rock.

"Looky, Grampy, I'm going to slip in the rocks," Davy had cried as he slid into the dark cave.

Grampy went in after him and pulled the child back into the sunlight.

"Run get a lantern, sonny," said Grampy. "I reckon you're old enough to go in the cave."

Davy ran as fast as his legs would carry him. He grabbed the lantern from the back porch and took a few matches from the kitchen.

Pa was home then, and he had smiled when Davy explained why he needed the lantern.

Ma was churning on the back porch, and she looked on uneasily as Davy gathered his supplies.

"I don't like caves," she commented. "A little fellow like Davy has no business there."

"Let the child go," replied Pa. "There's no harm in it if his grampy is with him."

When Davy returned to the cave with the lantern, Grampy lit the wick and they squeezed into the narrow entrance. Davy's bare feet were chilled by the damp floor, and his flesh crawled at the thought of snakes that might lurk behind the rocks.

But he forgot his uneasiness when he saw the shelf of Indian treasures that his grandfather had collected. Grampy reached up and handed Davy an arrowhead half as large as his hand and another as small as his fingertip.

"These here little ones," Grampy told him, "were to shoot birds with, I've heard."

Grampy laid a dark gray tomahawk on the floor, and beside it he placed an odd disk-shaped stone. The round disk was slightly indented on either side.

Davy held the smooth, unmarred artifact in his hands and carefully examined the delicate piece of workmanship.

"What is it, Grampy?" he asked.

"I don't know, sonny, what it is. I figure it's something they played a game with. Maybe some strong Indian men threw it."

Before Davy's bedazzled eyes Grampy displayed a peace pipe, more arrowheads, bowls, tomahawks, hatchets, and paint mills in which the Indians ground herbs for making war paint.

Finally, from the farthest corner he drew out his greatest treasure.

"This," he told Davy, "is like nothing I've ever seen. Lots of folks have found relics here and there, plowed them up, or found them in caves. But I don't know anybody who ever saw or heard of anything like this."

In the dim lantern light Grampy displayed a curious vessel. It was only slightly larger than his hand. It was a bird's body carved of stone. A hollow spot formed a sort of dish in the bird's back.

Davy turned it carefully in his hand.

"Maybe it was a plaything for somebody about my size," he suggested.

"Maybe so. I could never figure it out. But now we've got to get out of here. Your Ma won't like it if we don't bring the water up soon."

But all this happened four years ago—when Davy was six. Now Davy couldn't go to the cave any more this year. He had promised his mother. If only Grampy could walk, they would soon find out all about that mysterious skeleton.

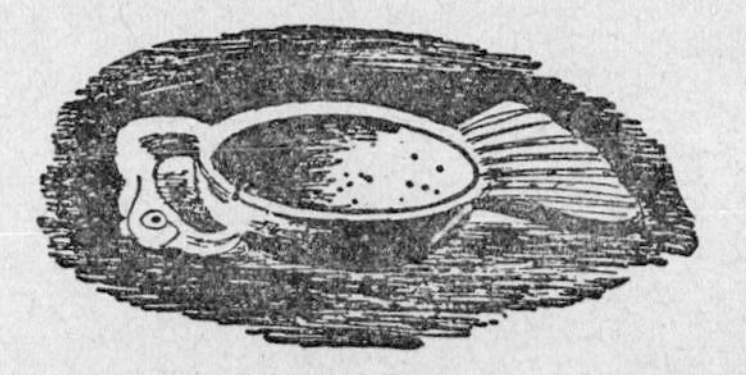

CHAPTER 4

SEVERAL DAYS after Davy discovered the skeleton, he trudged slowly downhill toward the spring, banging the empty water buckets against his legs. Ma liked the spring water for drinking, although they had a well on the back porch.

It was hard to go to the spring, so temptingly close to the cave, and not even be permitted to look inside. But Davy had promised, and he tried not to think of the skeleton which lay in the cave.

Davy flopped on his stomach and lapped water from the spring like a thirsty puppy. He tossed a pebble in the still pool and watched his reflection break into a thousand rippling freckles. An old bullfrog chugged at the intrusion, and Davy grinned. After all, a boy couldn't be unhappy forever on a June day in Alabama.

His mother's voice sounded from the hilltop. Davy quickly filled the buckets and started toward the house. The water spilled in little rivers down his bare ankles. His mother approached him down the path.

"Here, son, I'll take one," she offered, taking one of the heavy buckets. "Davy, I'm sorry about the cave," she said slowly. "I know it's hard, boy, but you see why you have to wait 'til your pa comes home, don't you?"

"Yes, Ma," replied Davy in a low voice, "but if only we could get Grampy some new legs, why we could go all right."

"Well, that can't be, son, and now you run up old Bessie for milking. I'll take that other bucket."

Davy let Bessie into the cow shed and fetched the scalded pail that his mother had ready. As he pulled the milk from the cow in long, even strokes, it hit the bottom of the pail in a noisy rhythm.

If only he could find a way to get Grampy to the cave!

"Get Grampy to the cave, get Grampy to the cave, get Grampy to the cave." He made a little singsong in time with the streams of milk.

Davy looked about him, and suddenly he stared at the wagon. Could he take Grampy in the wagon? Of course not—how would he get up to the tall seat? The wheelbarrow? Now maybe he could put Grampy in the wheelbarrow. But no, Davy was not strong enough or steady enough to manage that.

Bessie switched her tail in Davy's face.

"Quit it, Bessie. I guess I'm through with you today."

Carefully he put the milk pail aside and let the cow into her stall for the night. Cow feed, water, latch the door. He was all set.

"Goodnight, Bessie," he patted her nose.

"Moo," answered Bessie.

Mrs. Cobb had supper ready on the big table in the hall when Davy came in from the barn with the milk.

"Just set it on the well," said Mrs. Cobb, "and I'll tend to it after supper."

Davy helped Grampy get slowly to the table and into his chair. The three sat in the cool, wide hall that ran through the center of the house and separated the bedrooms on one side from the kitchen and "front room" on the other side.

Davy drank a glass of buttermilk, ate a helping of corn bread and meat, and asked for a second plate of turnip greens. Nothing tastes better than fresh tender greens from the garden, he told himself.

"I'm glad I kept the weeds out of these," said Davy. "I hope we'll be having some corn soon."

After supper Davy helped his mother with the milk. Some was strained into the churn and covered with a clean cloth. The rest went into freshly scalded glass bottles which were stored in the refrigerator. They were lucky to have the ice truck come this way once a week.

The warm Alabama twilight lasted long after the day's work was over. Davy sat down on the edge of the porch and began looking at the mail-order catalog. He thumbed through the pages, passing over pictures of baby clothes, dresses, suits, coats, girls' shoes. He idly looked at the boys' shoes, then glanced at his bare feet.

"I don't need shoes," he grinned, wiggling his bare toes in freedom.

The cowboy shirts he looked at with some longing, but he knew there was no money for such foolishness. Furniture, dishes, jewelry, he passed over.

"Now," he breathed as he turned to the worn section of the old catalog, "here's something I like."

He had found a page with pictures of farm equipment. He saw chicken feeders, beehives, pails, horse collars. There were tractors, plows, hoes, and rakes. The evening breeze ruffled the pages of the catalog.

"Hey, old wind, you lost my place," cried Davy as he put his hand out to still the fluttering pages. Right under his hand, instead of the plow he had been studying, was a picture of a chair. It had two big wheels and two little wheels. What a funny chair! Davy examined it closely.

Grampy was reading the county newspaper and paying no attention.

Suddenly Davy leaped up and thrust the catalog under Grampy's nose.

"Look, look!" the boy shouted in excitement.

Ma came running from the kitchen. Grampy settled the thick catalog in his lap, and the three gazed at Davy's discovery.

"Don't you see? If Grampy had one of these chairs, he could ride all around. He could go to the cave. Let's get Grampy a rolling chair!" Davy was jumping up and down with the pleasure of his wonderful idea.

Mrs. Cobb turned away.

"It's just a wheel chair, Davy. Anyhow, it costs $54.50. Where would we ever get $54.50 now?"

Davy let his shoulders droop. Of course, where would they get that much money?

Grampy was looking at the picture with patience and interest.

"It does look interesting, mighty interesting, Davy," said Grampy kindly. "Maybe when your pa is well and things go better on the farm, why then we'll be talking about rolling chairs. Right now, you've got to help your ma, Davy, and not let her be worrying about my legs. I don't mind it, to sit here. I've got my Bible and my newspaper, and I've got you, Davy. Let's not say any more about the chair. Help me to bed now. It's getting dark."

CHAPTER 5

IT WAS a good thing that Grampy had his newspaper. *The Citizen* was a county paper that came once a week, was ten pages long, and contained all the news that Grampy wanted to read. It told of the social activities of the various communities in the county. It told farm news, national news, and interesting facts about faraway places.

There was a page of funnies, and one of school news, and it told who died and who had new babies. Sometimes there would be very interesting local news, such as the time the Conners' cow had a two-headed calf, and the time the Whittingtons grew a sweet potato that weighed nine pounds.

The rural mail carrier put the paper in the Cobbs' mailbox down by the road every Tuesday morning, and Grampy would always look it over quickly that day. On the following days he would read it again more carefully. And by the time the week was over, he would have read every word in *The Citizen.*

Grampy read his Bible, too, holding the heavy, worn volume in his lap.

"Grampy, I bet you know that Bible by heart now," Davy would tease.

Sometimes Grampy would take his pocketknife and carefully cut important items from the paper. These he would use for bookmarks in the Bible and keep to read over later.

Grampy sat in the sun and read the second page of *The Citizen* again. Mrs. Cobb stuck her head out the front door to see if her father was all right.

"Need anything, Papa?" she asked.

"Not a thing, thank you," replied Grampy. "I'm always happy with my paper. I've found something in the paper about Indian relics," he added.

"Oh, that," said Mrs. Cobb. "Papa, I don't want Davy talking about that cave." Indian relics meant the cave to her.

"This isn't about a cave, daughter. I know you told him not to go without me. But it won't do any harm to let him seek for arrowheads a bit, out in the fields. Not all places have Indian relics like we do," he continued. "There were lots of Indians here once, before they were driven out. They were called Cherokees."

"I don't care about that," replied Mrs. Cobb. "Don't show that thing to Davy, please," she begged the old man, who was waiting to share this very interesting item he had found in the paper.

"All right, daughter," he sighed.

He placed the small clipping inside his Bible as Mrs. Cobb disappeared inside the house.

"Maybe she's right," he mused, "but maybe she's wrong," he added.

He looked again at the scrap of paper and read:

RELICS WANTED

The Anthropological Foundation is sponsoring a contest for the best hitherto unexhibited collection of Indian artifacts among Alabama collectors. All collections must be brought to the museum of Old South College in Birmingham. Dr. Richard Q. Moore, Foundation representative, will judge the collections during the week of July 7-14. For further information contact Dr. Thomas Durham, Geology Department, Old South College. The College will be responsible for all relics exhibited. A prize of fifty dollars will be given the most representative collection.

Grampy put the clipping back inside the Bible. If Davy just happened to find it in the Bible, why his mother couldn't blame him for that. Grampy had only promised not to *show* it to Davy.

Maybe it would be best if Davy never saw it, though. How would he ever get all his arrowheads and dishes to the College anyhow?

"What would I do if I were a boy Davy's size?" wondered Grampy. "Why, somehow I'd get those relics to Birmingham. And I believe Davy will, too."

Grampy began to smile. Davy was quite a boy. The first thing was to let Davy discover the news of the contest by himself. Grampy began to lay a small plot . . .

CHAPTER 6

"SONNY, don't be sad," Grampy said kindly to Davy, who sat with a drooping back turned toward his grandfather.

Davy kicked his legs against the side of the house and didn't answer.

"Did you ever hear of reading the Bible to solve your troubles, son?"

For an answer Davy continued to kick his feet in a dejected rhythm. What could the Bible tell him but to mind his mother, and he was doing that anyhow.

"Come read to me, Davy," requested the old man.

Davy rose heavily, pulled up a straight chair, and took the Bible into his lap.

"What shall I read, Grampy?" he asked.

"Oh, read me a psalm," suggested Grampy. He closed his eyes and leaned back in his chair.

Davy thumbed through the psalms, stopping now and then to look at the many clippings that served as bookmarks.

"Grampy!" Davy sat up very straight and spoke rapidly. "Looky here! Here's something about—"

"Davy," interrupted Grampy, "if you're going to try to talk to me about something your ma has told us not to, then you better get to reading the psalms."

"Yes sir," Davy replied. Quickly he read through the Twenty-third Psalm.

"Thank you, Davy," said Grampy at last. "Now if there's anything else in the Bible you'd like to read to yourself, go right ahead. I'll just sit here and take a nap in my chair."

Davy looked hard at Grampy, who was apparently drowsing. Ma stepped onto the porch and glanced approvingly at the quiet sight before her.

Davy read the clipping over twice. There was no

doubt that it was intended for him. He knew, he *knew,* that if he could put all the Indian relics in a big box and get them to the college in Birmingham, he'd win the prize! Then he could buy Grampy the wheel chair and they could go to the cave and investigate the skeleton.

Carefully Davy replaced the clipping in the Bible and laid the volume on the chair beside Grampy. Yes, if he could get the relics to town and win the prize, he could come pushing the wheel chair up the road and set Grampy right in it and just push him all around the farm!

But he'd promised Ma he wouldn't go to the cave, and he couldn't get the relics out without going in to get them. He couldn't even talk to Grampy about it. Anyway, even if he could get the relics out of the cave, how would he ever get them to Birmingham?

Right now Davy decided to go lie by the spring and try to think of a way.

CHAPTER 7

DAVY pondered his problem for two weeks as he went about his work. He turned it over in his mind while he milked Bessie. He sat silently at the table and ate without putting his mind on his food.

After supper he would sit quietly on the edge of the porch and watch the sun go down and the lightning bugs begin to make sparks in the twilight. Gradually he had come to the conclusion that it would be impossible to get the relics out of the cave and get them to Birmingham.

But he felt he might have a chance if he could only talk to the judges. After all, Grampy had said that the bird bowl was so rare that he never even knew of anyone who had heard of such a thing.

"Davy doesn't seem like himself," Mrs. Cobb admitted to Grampy with some concern.

She placed her hand on Davy's forehead and declared he wasn't feverish. She looked at his tongue and decided he did not need calomel.

"I guess he's fretting about the cave. I think I'll send him down the valley today to get me an embroidery pattern from Mrs. Tidwell. Maybe he can stay and play with the boys for a spell. I'll do his milking for him."

Davy was delighted. Mrs. Cobb insisted that he put on clean overalls and a shirt. He washed his face and slicked his hair down and set out whistling happily for a change.

The Tidwell boys were older than he, but they were glad to see Davy. They took him down to their pasture to a laden mulberry tree. The boys ate the sweet fruit and painted purple circles around their mouths with the juice.

"We're clowns," laughed James Tidwell. "I saw one once at a circus in Birmingham."

"We're going to Birmingham this week," bragged Amos, the younger boy.

"Really?" Davy looked at his friend with awe and surprise. "How come?"

"Pa's going to take a load of garden truck in to the Curb Market," explained James. "And you, Amos, you know Pa said you weren't going. He said there wouldn't be room in the truck."

"Maybe I'll hide," said Amos defensively. "Maybe I'll stow away."

"And you know what Pa would do if you did, don't you?" reminded James, with an older brother's righteous air. "Pa's taking me this time. You get to go next time."

"I wish I could go," sighed Davy.

The three boys walked back to the barn and looked over the pickup truck that was to make the trip to town.

"You see, it isn't big," said James, "but we load it carefully. We're going to put the melons on the bottom, and the light baskets of beans and greens and corn on top. Eggs go in front with Pa and me. I'll help Pa take the money when we sell the things.

One reason Pa doesn't want to take us both, he says one boy tends to business and two boys tend to play. I'll get to watch the truck by myself when Pa goes to the cafe for his coffee before we unload."

Davy was examining the truck and listening to the arrangements carefully.

"When do you aim to go?" asked Davy.

"We mean to get away about four next Friday morning. We'll pack the truck Thursday night. By then there'll be lots of stuff ripe. Friday's the best day to sell vegetables, they say." James prattled on about the wonders of the city.

"I've been to Birmingham, too," said Davy, "but it was a long time ago."

It was getting late when Davy finally collected the embroidery pattern from Mrs. Tidwell and set out for home. His mind was buzzing with ideas.

During his solitary walk home he worked out a daring plan. He would hide in the Tidwells' truck sometime Thursday night or Friday morning. He thought he could hide himself among the melons, beneath the lighter baskets, so that in the dim, early morning departure they would not notice him. When the truck reached Birmingham he could steal away while Mr. Tidwell went to the cafe for his coffee.

Of course he had to leave word for Grampy and Ma not to worry about him. He examined his conscience uneasily. Nobody ever told him *not* to go to Birmingham. All he wanted to do was to get to Old South College and find that professor man and tell him about the Indian relics.

When he finished with that he'd go back to the Curb Market. Mr. Tidwell would be plenty mad, but he couldn't refuse to take Davy home. There would be lots of room in the truck going back.

It was lucky that he had the two dollars he had earned selling blackberries in May. He would have to have some money with him. He'd have to get his shoes and his Sunday clothes out of Ma's room and have them ready to put on without letting anyone know. And he only had three days left to work out all the details!

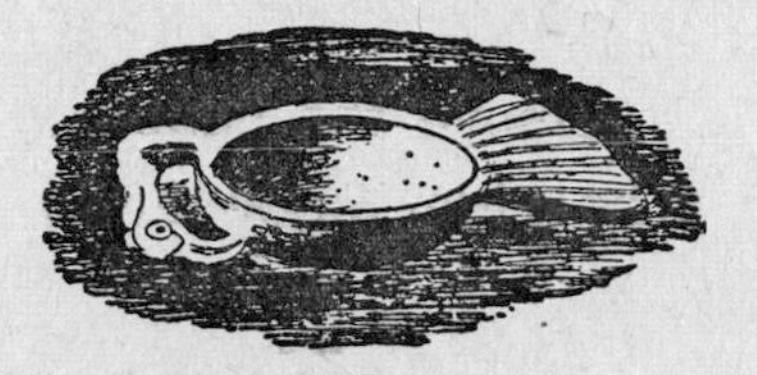

CHAPTER 8

DAVY'S SHOES and his good pants and shirt stayed in the big dresser in Ma's bedroom. Davy figured that he could quietly take them out and hide them in his room, in the wooden box that held his extra overalls. Then they would be ready to put on Thursday night.

His money was in the china box beside the clock on the mantel. It would be easy to have that all ready in his pants pocket.

The note was more of a problem. He could hardly decide what to write. Laboriously he composed a short message on a sheet of lined paper as he sat by the spring next day. He would put the note in Grampy's Bible before he left, and at the same time he would remove the clipping to take with him. Otherwise he might forget the name of the professor.

"Dear Ma and Grampy," he wrote. "I have gone to see about the prize. I will be back. I did not go in the cave. Davy."

He could not put the note in the Bible for two more days, but he must hide it carefully. He folded it into a small square and slid it into a crack in the wall behind the wooden headboard of his bed. Ma would never spy it there.

The clothes were difficult to manage. It seemed like Ma would never leave the house while Davy was there. Or if she did leave, Grampy was sitting up wide awake, looking in the porch window that opened into Ma's room.

All day Tuesday passed with no opportunity for getting the clothes out of the dresser. On Wednesday morning Davy was weeding the garden when Ma came out to pick greens for dinner.

"Davy, run fetch me my sun hat," asked his

mother. "If it's not on the back porch, it's on my dresser."

Davy ran like a rabbit to his mother's room. Grampy's chair was turned slightly away from the window. Davy quickly reached in the bottom drawer and drew out his small stack of good clothes. Luckily the sun hat was still on the dresser.

"That you, Davy?" asked Grampy, peering over his shoulder.

"Yes, sir, just getting Ma's sun hat," replied Davy.

He stepped into his shed room at the back of the house and slipped the clothes into the bottom of his box. Then he ran to deliver the hat to Ma.

"You were quick," she said as she stuck the hat on her head.

"Yes'm." Davy was panting with excitement, but Ma blamed it on his running.

"Don't run so hard this hot weather, Davy," she cautioned him. "You've been acting queer lately. I don't want you coming down with anything."

Davy pulled weeds intently and did not answer. His heart was pounding at the mere thought of the adventure that he was to undertake the next night.

On Wednesday afternoon Davy went over his plans again. He would wash thoroughly before supper Thursday night. That would make him clean enough. When Grampy was through reading the Bible after supper, Davy could slip the note in and take out the clipping at the same time. His clothes were ready to be put on, lying in the bottom of his box. He would go to bed as usual but not to sleep. As soon as Ma and Grampy were asleep, he'd dress and slip out.

Thursday dragged along slowly. When Davy brought the milk bucket up to the house late in the afternoon and set it down on the well, his mother reminded him to get washed up for supper.

"I declare, Davy," said his mother, "I don't think you'd ever wash if I didn't tell you."

Davy wanted to laugh aloud. This was one night when he wouldn't have to be reminded, but he wasn't going to tell his mother that. He doused his head in the washpan and soaped his ears and elbows. He poured the pan of water over his feet and dried himself on the rough towel that hung on the well curbing.

"Well I must say," Mrs. Cobb remarked, "you did a good job of it tonight."

After supper they sat on the porch to watch the sun set.

"I think I'll patch that pair of overalls of yours

that's in your box, Davy," said Mrs. Cobb, beginning to rise.

"I'll get 'em, Ma," cried Davy, leaping to his feet.

"What's got into him?" his mother asked Grampy.

Davy returned with the torn overalls and his mother's sewing basket. Phew, that was a close call! What if she had found his good clothes in the box?

When she finished mending the torn knee, Davy returned the overalls to the box.

The light was growing dim now, and Grampy had laid aside his Bible.

"I'll put it up for you, Grampy," offered the boy.

Grampy peered at Davy. The boy was mighty jumpy tonight.

Davy took the book and laid it on the hall table.

"Guess I'll go to bed," he called.

In his back room he took the note from its hiding place in the wall. He'd have to get the note in and the clipping out before it was dark, or he couldn't see what he was doing. He stepped quietly back into the hall, listened carefully, put his hand on the Bible and started to open it at Psalms, where he knew the clipping lay.

"Guess we better go in, too," he heard his mother say and the legs of her chair scraped the rough boards of the porch floor. Davy trembled as he fumbled for Psalms.

Ah, there it was! He slipped the clipping into his pocket and laid the note in the pages, just as his mother entered the hall with Grampy on her arm.

Davy stepped into his room, peeled off his overalls, and fell into bed in his underwear.

He lay still on his bed and answered his mother's "goodnight" when she stuck her head in the door. It was quite dark now, and Ma had lit a lamp. Must be she was going to sit up a while.

Somehow, it happened. Lying there in the cool dark, waiting for the house to get quiet, Davy fell asleep. He woke up as the clock on the mantel struck two. He sat up quickly, waiting to see if the clock would strike again. Two o'clock! He had a long walk to make before he got to the Tidwells' and hid himself in the vegetable truck.

Suddenly he was struck with the terrors of walking down the valley road at night, of prowling in the dark to the truck, and of all the chances of failure and detection that he might meet. He wanted to snuggle back under the quilt and forget it all. But he remembered the wheel chair and the cave.

With one great surge of courage he rose, feeling

for the flashlight under his pillow, and crept stealthily to his box for his clothes.

He pulled on his good pants and shirt, stuffed his clean socks into his shoes. He patted the money and clipping in one pocket and stuffed the flashlight into the other. His shoes he carried in his hand.

The night was chilly, and he reached back into his box for a raggedy sweater that he kept there. He fumbled in the dark for the comb that stayed on his shelf. He might need to comb his hair before he got to the College.

Although Davy could have unhooked the kitchen door and crept out, he thought it would not be right to leave the door unlatched for the rest of the night. As his window was close to the ground, he chose that means of leaving the house. He pushed his screen out gently, but it made a scraping sound that rasped like thunder to Davy.

He stood utterly still, and his heart raced as he heard Grampy turn heavily in his creaking bed. Davy waited a few seconds, but there was no more noise. Quietly he eased out the window to the ground below, shutting the screen very softly behind him.

As he crept across the yard the moon was dark, and the night was stiller than any stillness he had ever heard. He wished he had something to eat, and thought longingly of the cold biscuits that probably lay on the kitchen table.

He was passing by the garden now, and he remembered the vine-ripened tomatoes that hung there, ready for picking in the morning. He made a brief detour into the tomato patch and selected six soft ones.

Finally he set off, half scared, half relieved, at a slow trot down the dark valley road to Tidwells' farm.

CHAPTER 9

WHEN Davy had rounded the bend and was out of sight of the house, he turned on his flashlight and paused a moment to bite into a cold tomato. He felt more like walking after he had eaten two of them. The rest he put into his big sweater pocket.

He moved along at a half-trot, shining his flashlight on the road ahead. Once his light picked up a pair of eyes gleaming from under the low brush on the roadside. He stopped, terrified, thinking it might be a wildcat. But it was only the old, half-tame, gray tabby that caught mice in their barn.

"Kitty, kitty," called Davy, glad of her company. But she slithered away into the woods, as if to say she would have nothing to do with this secret midnight venture.

When he became more accustomed to the night and the loneliness, he switched off his light to save the battery. He could easily find his way on the familiar white dirt road. Before he reached Tidwells' he stopped to eat another tomato. Then he cautiously approached the fence to their property.

Davy walked carefully along the outside fence line, beyond the farmhouse, and around the barn. He knew the truck would be in the open place halfway between the barn and the house. He decided to approach from the barn.

All was still as he came through the barnyard. The outline of the truck stood out as a black lump in the dark gray horizon. He walked quietly and slowly toward it.

Suddenly he heard a low growl. It was Shep, the Tidwells' watchdog. Davy froze in his tracks. He had forgotten about the dog!

In the house someone stirred restlessly in a

squeaky bed. The sound carried through the night's still air. Would Shep's growl carry equally well?

"Here, Shep," whispered Davy. Maybe if he would pat the dog and identify himself as a friend, he might avoid a round of barking.

Shep stood stiffly, sniffing Davy. The boy crept forward to pat the dog's shaggy head. Shep relaxed and licked Davy's hand.

Cautiously Davy moved toward the truck. From the looks of the sky, it would soon be time for the Tidwells to get up.

Davy climbed on the rear bumper and surveyed the piles of fresh vegetables. He knew the melons were on the bottom. He moved along the wooden side of the truck, peering over at the baskets of corn, greens, and beans.

Finally he stepped nervously into a small toe hold, lifted a basket of corn, shifted a basket of beans, pushed over some of the melons. By wiggling and shifting and stacking and bracing he managed to make himself a comfortable little cubbyhole.

"I'm all curled up like a corn-silk bug," he thought to himself.

It wasn't too uncomfortable. The baskets of beans

which covered him were light, and it was warm on the floor of the truck.

It wasn't daylight, and Davy was tired from his long walk. In a very few minutes he was sound asleep among the vegetables in the back of Tidwells' truck.

He was awakened by the sound of Mr. Tidwell's voice calling to James.

"Bring the eggs, James," called the deep voice. "Lay them in front. The back's all set. Get the pie your ma baked for our dinner."

Davy held his breath. It was still not daylight. If Mr. Tidwell would just get on his way before day came, there would be little chance of Davy's being detected. Evidently Mr. Tidwell had taken a quick look over the back of the truck before Davy woke up.

"Lucky I don't snore," thought Davy, grinning to himself.

James arrived with the eggs, and Amos followed with the pie. Mrs. Tidwell came to watch the departure. She flashed a big flashlight over the vegetable baskets.

"Why don't you shift the beans nearer the front so they won't get so much dust," suggested Mrs. Tidwell, letting the light play over the vegetables.

"Well," said Mr. Tidwell, and Davy trembled beneath the baskets, "aw, no, May. They're all packed. They'll be all right. There's no dust this time of day."

"If you say so," Mrs. Tidwell reluctantly agreed.

"I say let's go, James," replied Mr. Tidwell as he got into the driver's seat.

After several tries that made Davy tingle with fear and excitement, the motor finally turned over and the truck began slowly to move over the bumpy yard into the road.

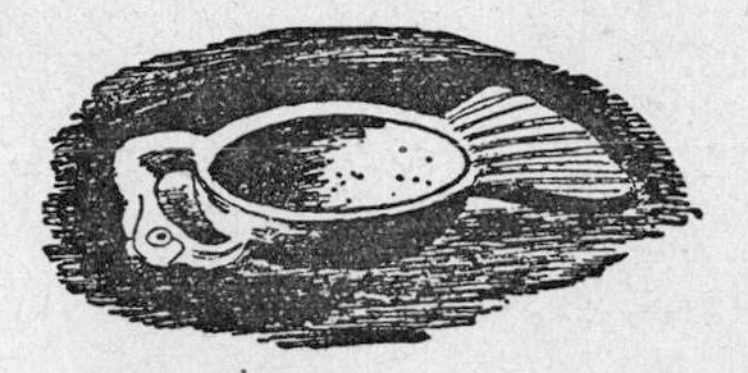

CHAPTER 10

DAVY joggled and jolted among the melons, sometimes sleeping, occasionally stretching his cramped arms and legs. He found that he could see a little through the slatted sides of the truck.

It was a bright sunny morning when they reached the outskirts of Birmingham. Davy felt for his socks and managed to get them on his feet. It was harder to get the shoes on. But Davy knew he must be ready to leave the truck the minute it was parked.

As the truck stopped for a traffic signal the motor stalled. A horn behind honked impatiently. Davy tried to lie small and still. They were so near the end of the journey that he prayed hard nothing bad would happen now.

"Need some help?" A blue-coated policeman stepped toward the truck.

Davy trembled with the thought of what would happen if they found him there.

The motor gave a chug and a sputter and began to turn. The policeman waved them on, and Davy let out a great sigh.

Past streetcars and busses, past houses and stores, past schools and churches, past shops and factories they drove. Davy got a fleeting picture of the city as they drew nearer the market.

They passed through a dark tunnel and back into the blinding sun. When they drove alongside several other trucks loaded with farm products, Davy braced himself. He knew they must be nearing the Curb Market.

With a clatter they pulled up and parked. After Mr. Tidwell cut off the motor, Davy's heart pounded like the motor's echo.

The market was filled with early morning noises of preparation for the day's selling. Davy could hear Mr. Tidwell open the door and step onto the sidewalk.

"I guess I'll look around a minute, maybe get me some coffee," Davy heard him remark. "Guess you can manage the truck, James?"

"Yes, sir," answered James briskly. He was proud to be in charge of the truck and the fine vegetables. "Shall I start to unload her?"

"Well, you might open up the back and pull out some of the baskets," replied his father. "There won't be any selling this early."

Davy lay motionless while Mr. Tidwell strolled down the sidewalk. James climbed on the back bumper and loosened the chain that held up the tail gate.

There wouldn't be a chance of escaping James' notice, but Davy thought he could count on his friend to help him. Davy cautiously raised the basket of beans that partially covered his face.

"Hey, James," he whispered.

James paused and looked behind himself.

"Hey, James," Davy whispered again.

This time James looked in the direction of the

voice. His eyes popped and his mouth opened, but no sound came forth.

Davy pushed the beans aside and sat up and laughed.

"Wh-what are you doing here?" gasped James.

"James, you've got to help me." Davy became sober at once. "Help me out of here, and don't tell your pa. I may be back to ride home with you, but I don't know if I'll get finished with my business in time."

James still stood with his mouth wide open, staring at Davy.

"Your business?" he croaked. "If Pa found you here you'd have some real business."

"James, don't tell," hissed Davy. "If you won't, I'll tell you a secret about a skeleton when I get home—if everything works out all right."

"Honest?" James still regarded Davy with astonishment.

"Get me out of here. Is your pa out of sight?" begged Davy.

"He's in the cafe across the street. I see his back," said the bewildered James. He moved a few baskets to let Davy out of the truck.

Davy was stiff from lying in the small space, but

4-2833

he had to move fast. His feet tingled as he jumped off the truck.

"Be seeing you, James. I want to leave my sweater in your truck. I don't aim to tote that raggedy thing all over Birmingham with me. So long."

Davy ran as fast as he could to the corner, where he turned and went two blocks without stopping. By now he must be safe from the danger of Mr. Tidwell.

On the corner an ice cream vendor was making ready for his day's work. Davy's stomach felt very empty. His remaining tomatoes were in the sweater in Tidwells' truck. He felt in his pocket for his money.

"What do you charge for ice cream," Davy asked politely of the ice cream man.

"Six cents," he replied.

"I'll take one," said Davy, importantly counting out his pennies.

"Little early for ice cream, isn't it?" laughed the man.

"Not for me," answered Davy. "Do you know how to get out to Old South College?"

"College, is it?" teased the vendor. "Aren't you a little young to go to college?"

"No, sir, I'm not too young for what I'm going

for," he replied seriously. "I just want to know what streetcar to take."

The ice cream man pushed his little white hat back on his head and thought deeply.

"Well, I think if you'll just walk over two blocks that way, and go left a block, you can find a bus labeled 'College.' "

Davy followed the pointing finger with his eyes. The fear of losing his way in the strange town made him shiver.

"Thank you, sir," said Davy, and he started off in the direction of the bus.

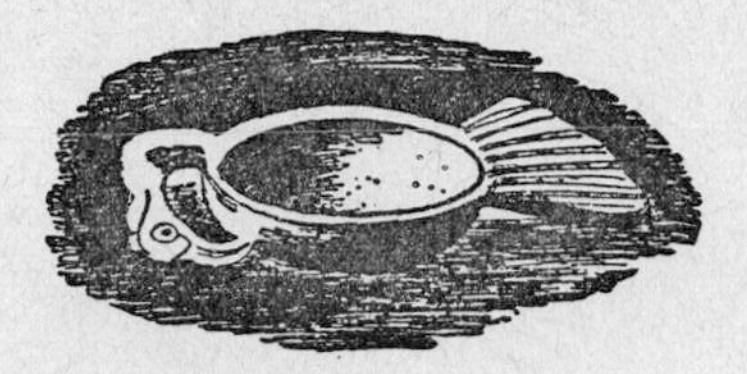

CHAPTER 11

DAVY was a little more scared in his walk through downtown Birmingham than he was in his lonely midnight walk down the valley road. The sidewalks were hard and his shoes felt tight on his feet, which were accustomed to bare freedom on country soil.

He stopped at the street corners and crossed the busy intersections with the crowd. He followed the directions of the ice cream man to the right street. There were busses everywhere, on all four corners. Davy backed up against a store window to watch for a moment.

He was about to ask the newsman on the corner where to catch the bus when a big one swerved up to the curb in front of him. Its brakes screeched, its motor panted. Across the front Davy read the word "College."

Davy's shaky legs took him up the bus steps. He had never been on one in his life. The man before him had dropped some money into the glass box beside the driver. Davy hesitated.

"What'll it cost me?" he asked the driver.

"Fifteen cents," replied the man.

Davy carefully counted out two nickels and five pennies.

"Where're you going, son," asked the driver, looking at Davy curiously.

"To the College," Davy replied.

"Ever been there?"

"No, sir," answered Davy.

People behind Davy began to grumble at the delay.

"Sit there," the driver indicated the seat directly behind his own. "I'll tell you when to get off."

Davy sat down gratefully. Folks were pretty

nice, even in a big town like this. He settled back to look out the window. He was feeling fine now, with his ice cream to nourish him, a soft seat to sit in, and on the last lap of his journey.

He watched as the tall buildings in the downtown section were replaced by warehouses and factories. He perched on the edge of the seat and watched with excitement as they passed a foundry. It was making a run of pig iron that glowed like millions of red-hot pokers.

As the passengers thinned out, the bus passed houses and parks and vacant lots. Davy began to wonder if the bus driver had forgotten him.

"Please, sir," he asked, "when will we get there?"

"Oh, the College?" replied the driver. "Before long. I'll tell you."

Soon he began to see large buildings rising in the middle of a well-clipped green campus. The driver drew the big bus to the curb.

"College," he called.

Davy stepped off the low steps and watched the bus depart. Straight up the long drive before him was the big Administration Building. A flag was flying in front of it. Davy felt small and smaller as his eyes traveled up the hill and then up, up to the top of the flagpole.

His knees were weak, and his mouth was dry. He was here at last, and he was too scared to walk up the hill. If he had been told to climb to the top of the flagpole it would not have seemed more difficult.

A few people were strolling on the sidewalks around the campus. An ice cream truck turned into the driveway and crawled slowly up the hill. Davy watched while two summer-school students hailed the truck and the white-uniformed driver opened up the refrigerator.

Davy ran up the hill after it, forgetting his fear of the College in his haste to reach the truck. Panting, he bought an ice cream sucker and sat down on the low wall to eat it. The mid-morning heat made the ice cream deliciously cool.

All he had to do now was to find the professor. He drew the worn scrap of newspaper from his pocket. Suddenly he wondered if Grampy and Ma had found his note and if they were awful mad at him.

He wiped his mouth on the back of his hand and stood up. Taking a deep breath for courage, he marched up the steps of the Administration Building.

Davy walked down a long corridor. There were

many doors with names painted on them, but he saw none with "Dr. Thomas Durham" on it. Through the open doors Davy could see men busy at their desks.

He peeped in one door and was flustered when a bald-headed gentleman looked up and met his eyes.

"What is it, boy?" the man asked.

"Are you Dr. Thomas Durham?" Davy inquired, turning red.

"No, Dr. Durham is away this week, I think. Maybe his assistant is in. He'll be in the Science Building. Right over there." The man pointed to a building directly opposite.

Davy thanked him and walked down the hall and out into the sunshine again.

Dr. Durham gone, after all this trouble getting here! Davy wasn't sure what an assistant was, but maybe he could help.

CHAPTER 12

DAVY wandered into the Science Building and peered at the names on the doors. There were rooms of equipment where young men and women were busily at work. In other rooms people were sitting in chairs while a teacher stood in front, talking to them.

Then right before him there it was—a closed door with "Dr. Thomas Durham" printed on it! Davy knocked politely, and a voice asked him to come in.

Davy stood tongue-tied and stared at the man who was sitting at a desk.

"Yes, yes, boy, what is it?" the man asked a little impatiently.

"I wanted to see Dr. Thomas Durham," Davy faltered, "but I don't reckon you are him."

The man laughed and put down his pen. "What makes you think that? I am Dr. Durham."

"But, but—that other man said he was gone," replied Davy.

"Oh that. I just tell them that so I can work in peace. Who are you?" Dr. Durham asked, suddenly interested in the small, scared, country boy.

"I'm Davy Cobb," answered the boy, "and I came to ask you if I can enter the contest."

"Contest?" Dr. Durham looked puzzled.

"Yes, sir, the Indian relic one."

"Oh that. It's closed. Dr. Moore has already judged the entries."

Davy stared at the professor in disbelief. The contest couldn't be closed! He clinched his hands and tried to blink back the tears that started to form.

The cave seemed very far away. The cave which he had intended to enter in triumph, pushing Grampy in a fine new wheel chair. He wished he

were back on the porch at home, watching Grampy read the Bible.

He stumbled wordlessly from the small office into the hall. He felt he had to get away as fast as he could so no one would see the tears that were running freely down his cheeks. If only Ma were here! She would have a handkerchief with which he could wipe his eyes.

He was running now, and he ran faster when the voice boomed out behind him:

"Hey, boy! Hey, Davy, wait! I want to talk to you."

But Davy didn't wait. He wanted to get out the open door at the end of the corridor. It was over now. No contest, no wheel chair, no going to the cave until Pa came home.

A big hand dropped on his shoulder. Dr. Durham, winded by the chase, breathed heavily as he spoke:

"Come back here, boy. Tell me what you're up to." He produced a handkerchief and attempted awkwardly to wipe Davy's face.

Davy controlled his tears and followed the professor back to the office.

"Now," said Dr. Durham after he had seated Davy in a chair, "tell me what this is all about."

Davy told him from beginning to end about the cave and the wheel chair and how the skeleton and the Indian relics had washed up in the flood. And even about the trip to town under the vegetables in the back of Tidwells' truck. He told Dr. Durham about the secret shelf that held the bird bowl and the queer disk-shaped rocks and the tomahawks and the paint mills and the arrowheads.

The professor listened intently.

"But you see," ended Davy, "Ma won't let me go to the cave while Pa's gone and Grampy's sick. So I just thought, I just hoped, that if I told you about the things I might get the prize. Then I could buy the wheel chair, and Grampy and I could get the relics out and send them to you. Grampy and I could dig up the skeleton, too. We think he's an old Indian."

Dr. Durham fingered the telephone on his desk.

"Davy," he said, "although the contest is over, Dr. Moore is still in town. You and I are going to find him. Let me call his hotel now. Then you and I are going to get something to eat. How would you like to drive back to your home in my car, with Dr. Moore and me? You could show us the cave. Do you think your mother would let you go in the cave with us?"

"Yes, sir," Davy grinned until his freckled cheeks touched his eyes. "And I sure would like some dinner, like you said."

Dr. Durham grinned back at him as he dialed the hotel. Dr. Moore was in and promised to wait in the lobby until they arrived, so they could all have lunch together.

Davy followed Dr. Durham to his car and rode proudly beside him to the downtown hotel. His hungry stomach was rumbling like marbles in an empty barrel.

Davy was so awed by the high ceilings and the well-dressed people that he hardly listened as Dr. Durham introduced him to Dr. Moore. Dr. Durham began to tell Davy's story as they moved into the dining room.

When the waitress placed the menus before them, Davy looked at the list of food and thought that he was supposed to eat *all* of it. He had never seen a menu before.

"What will you have, Davy?" asked Dr. Durham.

"I don't care," blushed Davy.

The two men laughed.

"Bring this boy a hamburger and a glass of milk and some fried potatoes and ice cream," requested Dr. Durham.

Davy was relieved. He wasn't a bit sure he would have liked most of the strange dishes listed on the menu.

During lunch, Dr. Durham and Davy told Dr. Moore about the cave and about Grampy's collection of relics. While Davy described the bird bowl, Dr. Durham motioned the waitress to bring Davy another hamburger. The first one was so good that Davy had gulped it down. But he had noticed that the hotel milk wasn't nearly as rich as old Bessie's milk.

Dr. Moore had planned to leave the city that afternoon, but he rapidly changed his plans.

"I believe, Davy, that your cave and your collection will give me the very information the Foundation sent me to discover. Since Dr. Durham has so kindly offered to drive us out in his car, I think we might as well be on our way."

"Please sir," asked Davy hesitantly, "would it be too far to go by the Curb Market? I figure James Tidwell might like to know I got me another ride home."

Dr. Durham laughed and agreed.

"There's the truck," said Davy as they slowed up at the market.

"Hey, James!" he called through the window. "I got another ride home."

James looked up speechless, his mouth wide open with astonishment. He was still staring at the departing car when his father sauntered over.

"I declare, James, that looked like Davy Cobb in that car," remarked Mr. Tidwell.

"Yes sir, it sure did," James finally managed to speak. "A whole lot like him."

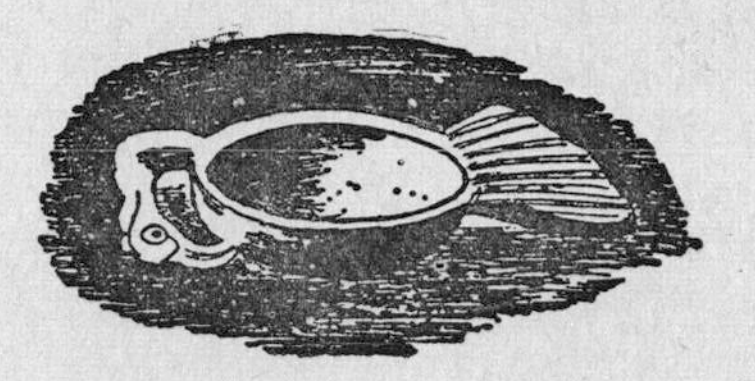

CHAPTER 13

WHEN the city was an hour and a half behind them, Davy proudly showed the men where to turn off the highway and which of the winding country roads to follow. As they approached the gate to the Cobb farm, Davy remembered uncomfortably that he was probably in disgrace with Ma and Grampy.

It was nearly four in the afternoon when the car stopped in front of the Cobbs' house. Grampy was

sitting in his chair on the porch as usual. Mrs. Cobb stood in the door in her hat and Sunday clothes.

At the sight of them Grampy began to smile and wave, but Ma broke into tears.

Davy ran to his mother, and they hugged each other tight for a moment.

"Did you find my letter in the Bible?" he asked, breaking the silence.

Mrs. Cobb nodded her head and continued to weep. "Where've you been, son?" she managed to ask.

"I told you, daughter, he'd be back." Grampy grinned at Davy. "I knew he'd be home before the sun set."

The two visitors stood awkwardly by the edge of the porch until Mrs. Cobb straightened up and dried her eyes.

"I was going to walk to the store and call the sheriff, but Papa here wouldn't let me go. You gentlemen have chairs," she said, recalling her manners, "and let me fetch you some cool water. We thank you for bringing Davy home, although we don't know how you came to do it."

Davy introduced his new friends, and Ma took off her hat and brought out the water.

When they were all settled on the porch, Davy

told about his ride to town in the Tidwells' truck, and how he had found the two men who had brought him home.

As Davy talked, Ma looked very stern, but Grampy was unable to control his smile. However, neither of them made any comment as Davy finished his story.

While Grampy and the visitors talked about the cave and the relics, Davy slipped into his room and took off his town clothes. He put on his old torn overalls and shirt. He wiggled his toes joyfully as he removed his hot shoes.

Davy eased back to the porch, not daring to enter the conversation. He still felt Ma's eyes staring at him.

"Please, Ma," he finally asked, "could I take the gentlemen to the cave?"

Ma slowly nodded her agreement. But before they set out she made the men agree to stay for supper.

"I'll get back in time to milk, Ma," promised Davy.

Ma ran her hand softly over the top of Davy's head, and he knew he was going to be forgiven.

CHAPTER 14

WITH his flashlight in his hand Davy led the way into the cave. There it sat, undisturbed —the skeleton that had scared Davy out of his wits only a few weeks ago.

Dr. Moore borrowed the light and made a quick examination of the skeleton. He made deft measurements with his fingers, dug slightly in the moist sand around the head of the figure.

"By jove, Durham, he's an Indian all right! The

skeleton is quite intact. I think this is going to be of help to me."

Dr. Durham was busily examining the relics which were stored on the shelf.

Dr. Moore straightened up and walked over to his friend. Together the two men looked over the

collection. They murmured to each other and occasionally let out a whistle or an excited exclamation.

"There must be more here, too, under the sand. I believe this cave must have been a tribal storehouse, so to speak. My guess is that the old fellow over there died defending the place." Dr. Moore pointed to the Indian remains in the sand.

"Rare pieces, rare pieces," exclaimed Dr. Durham. "If the Cobbs are interested in selling these things, I think they may find many collectors who would bid high for some of these specimens."

Davy stood silently by until the two men were ready to leave the cave. But he managed to get his courage up as they walked up the hill to the house.

"Will they win a prize—the skeleton and the dishes?" he asked timidly.

Dr. Moore laughed. "Well, Davy, the prize for the collection has been given. But you have here what we failed to find among the other collections —certain necessary relics that further the line of study being made by my Foundation. I have some of the Foundation money at my disposal. Not much, but enough to offer you a prize extraordinary."

By this time they had reached the porch, where Grampy and Ma were waiting for them eagerly.

"I don't know what that kind of prize means," confessed Davy.

"Well," said Dr. Moore, "it means that we can manage a prize sufficient to buy a wheel chair, which Dr. Durham tells me will cost $54.50."

When Dr. Moore finished his announcement, the speechless Davy walked to Grampy and laid his hand inside the old man's. He had no words for his joy.

"And," continued Dr. Moore, "with your mother's and grandfather's permission, we can probably pay a small sum for the privilege of making photographs and doing certain excavations in and around the cave. I feel that Grampy there in his wheel chair can be a lot of help to us."

Davy's head was swimming as he heard Ma and Grampy give permission.

"Davy," reminded his mother, "don't you forget about the milking."

"Yes, Ma," he replied as he ran off the porch toward the barn.

Old Bessie was mooing impatiently. As the milk filled the pail, Davy wondered what James Tidwell would think when he heard the whole story. He had an idea that James would come visiting early the next morning.

That evening the Cobbs and their visitors sat around the hall table, eating fresh corn, beans, tomatoes, and country-cured ham. Ma filled and refilled the milk glasses and the biscuit plate.

Dr. Durham confessed that he had lost count of the biscuits and sorghum he had eaten.

"You raise fine sorghum cane here," he remarked.

"Thank you, we like it," admitted Mrs. Cobb modestly.

"And you've raised a good son, too, Mrs. Cobb," added Dr. Moore. "He didn't disobey you by going in the cave, even though he had a boy's natural desire to see the skeleton again."

Davy's lowered eyes studied the empty plate before him. He was not used to so much attention.

"Thank you," replied Mrs. Cobb. "And now, Davy, don't you be getting the big head, or you won't be able to get it through the entrance when you go pushing Grampy down to Skeleton Cave in his new wheel chair."

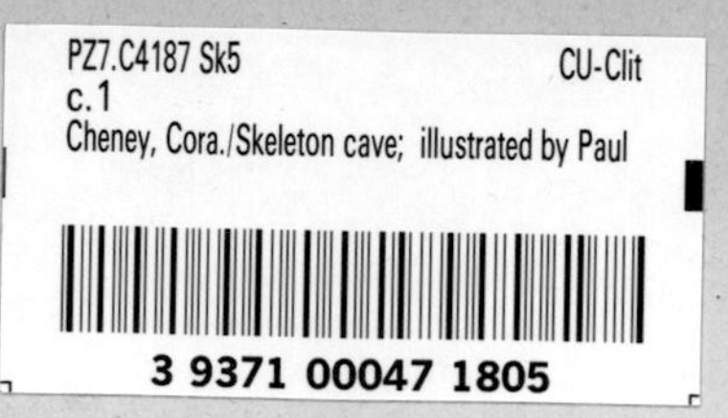